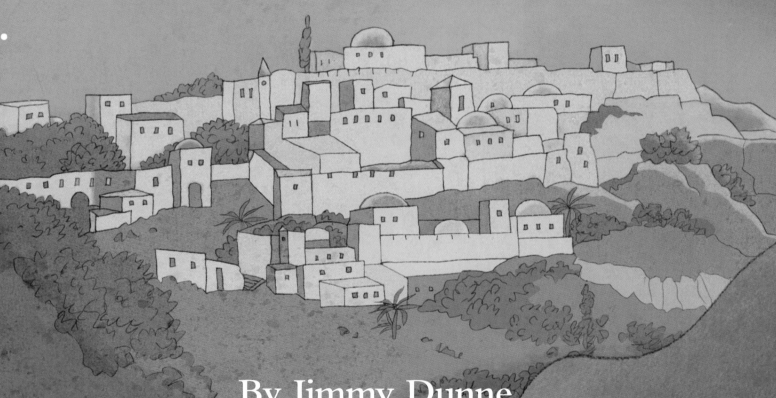

The
Shepherd's Story

By Jimmy Dunne

Illustrated by Ivan Kravets

LOYOLAPRESS.

LOYOLA PRESS.

3441 N. Ashland Avenue
Chicago, Illinois 60657
(800) 621-1008
www.loyolapress.com

ISBN: 978-0-8294-4890-0

Library of Congress Control Number: 2020931890

Printed in China

20 21 22 23 24 25 26 27 28 29 RRD 10 9 8 7 6 5 4 3 2 1

My Christmas wish for you . . .

Whether you're three or ninety-three,
may this poem remind you of that extraordinary light
that is always, forever, in you.
That light is your true treasure.
May you have the courage and will
to share it with the world.

—Jimmy Dunne

'Twas the very first Christmas, when all through the hills, the towns of Judea were *perfectly* still.

The sheep were all grazing – with only one care, hoping the wolves would *never* be there.

The Judeans were nestled all snug in their beds,
while visions of sweet figs danced in their heads.

I lay in the grass with my crook in my lap
and settled my brain for a quick little nap.

All alone with those sheep, night after night,
I'd get sad when I just couldn't see any light.

A shepherd is not what I thought I would be,
I just couldn't see any future for me.

When over the meadow there 'rose such a clatter,
I sprang from the grass to see what was the matter.

Next thing I knew, I saw a bright flash,
so I bolted from there in a hundred-yard dash.

When what to my wondering eyes should appear,
a glorious angel saying, "Nothing to fear ..."

8

"Do not be afraid. I bring news of great joy.
In the City of David, born is a boy."

9

"The Savior, Messiah, our Lord has been born.
This day will forever be called Christmas morn!"

The angel said, "Go now. The sheep aren't in danger.
Go find the babe sound asleep in a manger."

More angels appeared. They sang as a choir.
I felt underdressed in my dusty attire.

I looked at my lambs—they weren't lively or quick.
Their hooves were too tiny; their wool was too thick.

I held up my crook. This wasn't a game.
I whistled, and shouted, and called them by name.

"Now, Sheep 1! Now Sheep 2, Now Sheep 3 and Sheep 4!
Don't move from this hill, or I'm gonna be sore!

I need to go find this new baby somehow,
I'll dash away, dash away, dash away, now!"

I waved to my flock, off to B-town I hiked.
After seeing that angel, I had to be psyched.

After six miles of walking to reach Bethlehem,
I wondered just how I would *ever* find them.

And then, in a stable, beneath a thatched roof,
I heard the light clacking of an old donkey's hoof.

As I peered inside, what did I see?
A Mother and child. And a Dad smiled at me.

I knew in a moment this child was the one.
The life in the room was as bright as the sun.

Baby's eyes, how they twinkled! His dimples, how merry!
'Tho the beard on dear Joseph was a little too hairy.

And Mary, dear Mary. She looked up and smiled.
Life has no moment as the birth of a child.

Two things, I must say, took me quite by surprise—
the *quiet* in the room and the joy in their eyes.

What I felt on that morning—a vision so wild,
the *deep* love both parents had for their child.

Their faith gave them hope of what one child could bring—
the song in that child, no choir could sing.

How blessed are we all, that one child was born,
how blessed are we all on this great Christmas morn!

To imagine the good that one child can do . . .
If you've witnessed a birth, then you've felt it, too.

Today we give thanks for the wonder of life,
to the heart of a husband and the will of a wife.

To family, *sweet* family—a most precious word,
to the voice of a child that needs to be heard.

To the hope that one child, just *one* child can bring,
to the melody nature continues to sing.

I spoke not a word, but went straight on my way,
to share the good news that I saw on that day.

As I walked back that night, I stared up at the stars
and thought about how *truly* blessed we all are.

I got down on my knees to the wonder of life,
"Merry Christmas to all—and to all a good night!"